THE DENTIST FROM THE BLACK LAGOON

STORY BY
MIKE THALER

PICTURES BY
JARED LEE

Cartwheel
·B·O·O·K·S·®

SCHOLASTIC INC.

New York   Toronto   London   Auckland   Sydney
Mexico City   New Delhi   Hong Kong   Buenos Aires

To Dr. Solberg and Joanne,
only kidding!
—M.T.

To all the friendly dentists everywhere
who take good care of our teeth.
—J.L.

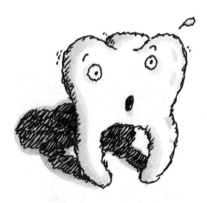

No part of this publication may be reproduced in whole or in part, stored in a retrieval system, or transmitted in any form or by any means, electronic, mechanical, photocopying, recording, or otherwise, without written permission of the publisher. For information regarding permission, write to Scholastic Inc., Attention: Permissions Department, 557 Broadway, New York, NY 10012.

ISBN-13: 978-0-545-07783-5
ISBN-10: 0-545-07783-4

Text copyright © 2005 by Mike Thaler.
Illustrations copyright © 2005 by Jared D. Lee Studio, Inc.

All rights reserved. Published by Scholastic Inc.
SCHOLASTIC, CARTWHEEL BOOKS, and associated logos
are trademarks and/or registered trademarks of Scholastic Inc.

Library of Congress Cataloging-in-Publication Data is available.

10 9 8 7 6 5 4 3 2 1   8 9 10 11 12 13/0
Printed in the U.S.A. · This edition first printing, September 2008

Uh-oh, it's Dental Health month!

SUN

Miss Hearse, the nurse, says there's a real dentist
coming on Friday. His name is Dr. B.N. Payne.

TOOTH FAIRY

He's bringing his equipment, and he's going to check our teeth.

ELLOW
BUG

AUNT

I don't want checked teeth…

maybe polka-dotted ones.

I'm scared! I heard all dentists have four hands, two heads, and are *Yank*-ee fans. After your teeth are taken out, they give you toothpaste to stick 'em back in.

TOOTHPASTE

YANKS

One kid said a dentist gave his cousin gas. I hope it was unleaded.

FILLING STATION

GAS

DRILL SERGEANT

TOOTHPICK

WE STRUCK OIL!

Then he drilled him.

Another kid said a dentist put *caps* on his brother's teeth.
His mouth must have looked like a Little League team.

Penny said her aunt has *crowns* on hers.

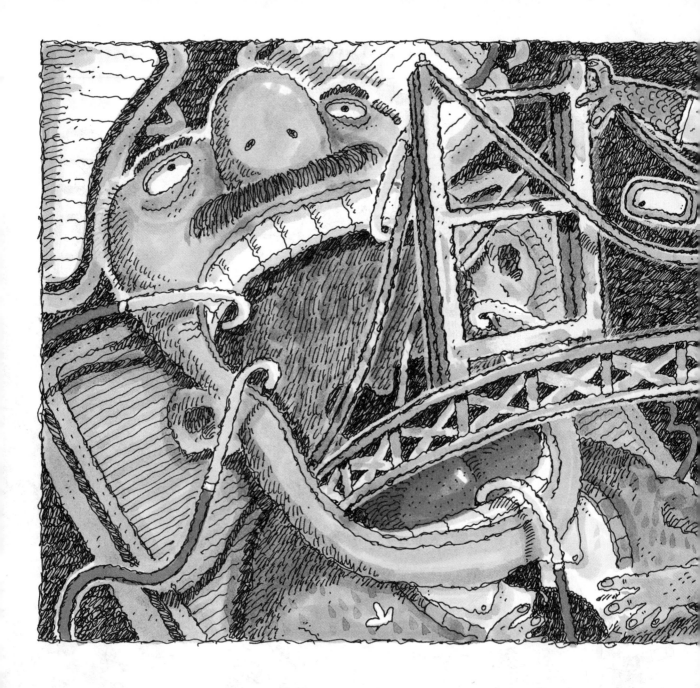

"Big deal," said Derek. "A dentist put a bridge in *my* uncle's mouth."

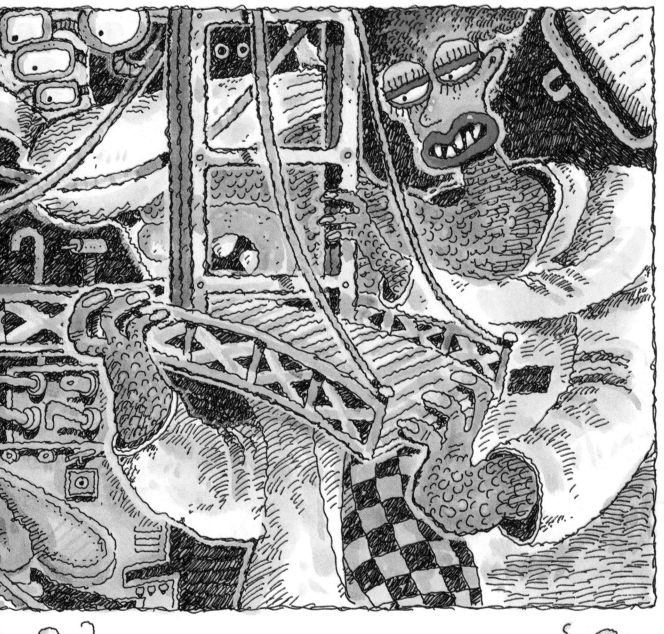

FLOSS

Wow, I hope it wasn't the Golden Gate!

NOODLE

He also said his dad has a whole root canal in his mouth—

sounds *Erie* to me.

My best friend, Eric, is going to a special dinosaur dentist called an *ORTHODON*, who's giving him a good bite.
I told him to brace himself.

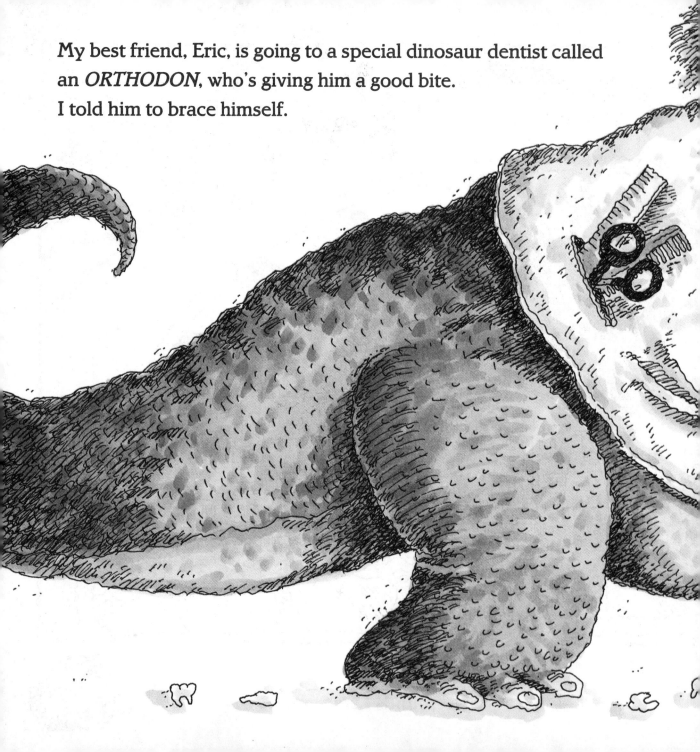

My grandpa told me my grandma's teeth are like stars—

they come out at night.

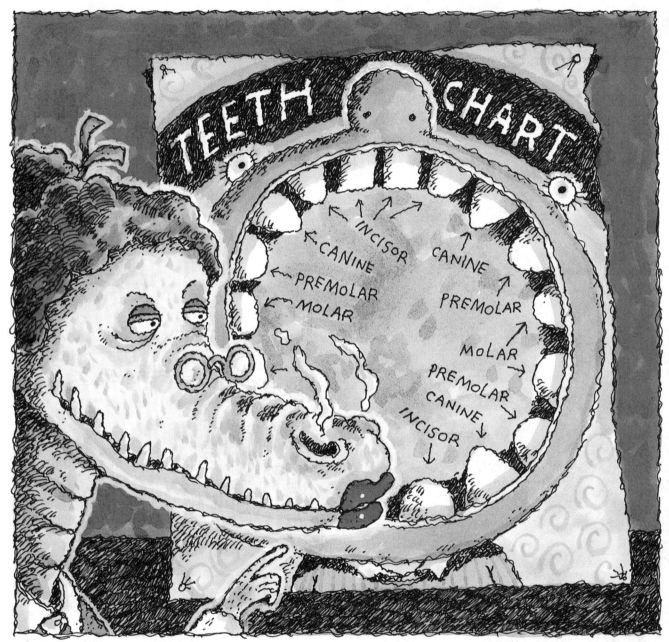

Mrs. Green says each tooth has its own name.

I thought they all had *my* name and were just called "Hubie's teeth."

MOLAR POWER

Well, *my* teeth are staying in *my* mouth!

SMILE

 I DON'T HAVE TEETH.

Oh, no, we're on our way to the nurse's office.

 EYE TOOTH

We line up by the door and go in—one by one.

I don't hear any screams *yet*. I'm polite and let everyone go ahead of me. But finally, it's *my* turn. . . .

I go in…there's a man in a mask sitting there.
And it isn't the Lone Ranger.

LONE RANGER →

Dr. Payne tells me to open wide and looks in my mouth with a little mirror. Then he pats me on the head, gives me a new toothbrush, and tells me to use it every day.

← BABY TOOTH

Hey, that wasn't so bad. I got out of there with all my teeth,
a new toothbrush, and a great big smile!